Copyright © Val Biro, 2001

The moral right of the author/illustrator has been asserted

First published 2001 by Happy Cat Books,
Bradfield, Essex CO11 2UT

A CIP catalogue record for this book is available from the
British Library

ISBN 1 903285 00 3 Paperback
ISBN 1 903285 01 1 Hardback

Printed in Hong Kong by Wing King Tong Co. Ltd.

THE JOKING WOLF

A Hungarian Folk-Tale
retold and illustrated by

Val Biro

Happy Cat Books

ONCE upon a time there was a farmer. A mean and greedy farmer – so greedy that he spent the winter indoors, eating six dinners a day. He got so fat that he looked like a tub of lard.

In the barn outside he kept a horse, a goat and a pig.
But he was so mean that he barely fed them.
The poor creatures were starving, and by the end of
winter they looked like bags of bones on legs.

One spring morning the farmer lost his temper.
'Look at you!' he yelled at the animals.
'Why didn't you fatten up last winter?
You are no use to me now, get out!'
and he flung open the gate.
'Let the wolf eat you for
all I care!'

Now, it so happened that a wolf was lurking nearby, and he heard the farmer. He was a hungry wolf, so when he saw the horse come out he skipped across and spoke.

'Let me eat you as the farmer said!'

The horse said, 'All right,
if you must. But you won't enjoy me
because I'm just a bag of bones. Let me go to
the hills where I'll graze all summer. When I return
I'll be so fat that you'll enjoy every mouthful.'
The wolf liked this idea and let the horse go.

Farther up the road he met the pig trotting along.
The wolf stopped her.

'Let me eat you as the farmer said!'

'If you like,' replied the pig. 'But look at me!
I am just a bag of bones. Now, if you can wait till
autumn, I shall be so fat that when I return –
with my fat little piglets, mind – you'll have a feast.'

The wolf rather liked the sound of fat little piglets, so
he allowed the pig to go on her way.

Just then the goat appeared and the wolf sprang
in front of him.

'Let me eat you as the farmer said!'

'By all means,' replied the goat, 'but I am only a
bag of bones just now. Wait till I return from the
hills this autumn and you can have a real dinner.'

He is right, you know, muttered the wolf to himself,
and he let the goat go, too.

The wolf spent the entire summer in preparation for his great autumnal feast. He kept dreaming about fat horses and round goats, he drooled at the thought of porky pigs and succulent piglets, all trotting down the hill towards his dinner table.

Autumn came at last. The wolf tried to guess who would be first. He could hardly wait.

The pig came first, with her six little piglets trotting behind. They were all as fat as barrels.

'Thanks for keeping your word,' said the wolf. 'Come, let me eat you now. I've been waiting for this all summer!'

'Yes, of course,'
replied the pig,
'but please wait for
just one more day.
The trouble is, you see,
there was no priest up in
the hills, so my piglets haven't
been christened yet. And I'm sure
you would not want to eat them even
before they've been given their names?'
The wolf agreed, because that would be too cruel.

The pig was grateful
and she winked at the wolf.
'Come near and let me
whisper their names
in your ear.'

Instead of whispering, the pig clenched her teeth around the wolf's ear and shook him and shook him until he cried out: 'Stop! Stop! I was only joking!'

But the pig went on shaking him, and the piglets joined in too, until they shook the wolf nearly out of his skin.

In the end the wolf managed to wriggle free and he was lucky to escape with his life.

The wolf had hardly got his breath back when the goat appeared.
The sight of a fat goat made the wolf forget that terrible shaking, and his mouth began to water again.

'I am glad you are so fat and ready to be eaten,' said the wolf. 'But don't you play a trick on me like that pig!'

'Why should I?' protested the goat. 'After all, I've fattened myself up just for you.'

The wolf was so grateful to hear this that he promised to eat the goat very gently.

'Thanks,' said the goat. 'Just open your mouth and I'll jump in so that you can swallow me whole.'

So the wolf opened his mouth wide and shut his eyes. The goat lowered his head and charged. But instead of jumping into his mouth...

…the goat butted the wolf so hard that it sent him flying.
The goat butted again and again, until the wolf cried out:
'Don't do that! I was only joking!'

So the goat jumped over him and ran away. The wolf
crawled into a bush to lick his wounds.

Soon the horse arrived, nice and fat. The sight made the wolf hungrier than ever.

'I am glad you've come back,' said the wolf. 'Come here, let me eat you munch-munch. I need my dinner!'

The horse nodded. 'You can eat me munch-munch, but first I must go to the village and carry the bride to her wedding. Then I'll come back and you can eat your fill.'

The wolf suspected a trick. 'I want to come too and see that bride for myself.'

'Very well,' said the horse. 'Get on my back.'

As soon as the wolf scrambled up, the horse shot forward at a gallop and they reached the village in no time.

A big crowd was there, all dressed for the wedding.

People were alarmed to see a wolf on a galloping horse. 'A wolf, a wolf!' they cried, 'here comes the wolf on horseback!' Some jumped to safety, but others grabbed sticks and brooms and dragged the wolf off his horse.

'Don't hit me!' howled the wolf, 'I was only joking!'
But they thrashed him biff-baff-biff just the same,
then chased him right out of the village. The wolf
could barely make his escape into the forest.

A woodman happened
to be working there.
All that hullabaloo made
him look up, and he was
alarmed to see a panting
wolf loping towards him.
So he hid behind the
trunk of a tree.

The wolf was exhausted, so he hid behind the same tree – but on the other side. He'd been tricked again, for the third time. 'Serves me right,' he moaned, 'for being such a fool. I deserve to be knocked on the head!'

'Well, if that's what you want,' said the woodman,
'take this!' And he knocked the wolf on the head, thump!
'But I was only joking!' protested the wolf as he staggered
away, head spinning, to a safe distance.

'Really,' he thought, 'what's the world coming to when people can't take a joke any more?'